P9-DVQ-652

TORTILLITAS PARA MAMA

TORTILLITAS PARA MAMA

And Other Nursery Rhymes

Spanish and English

selected and translated by
MARGOT C. GRIEGO, BETSY L. BUCKS,
SHARON S. GILBERT and LAUREL H. KIMBALL

illustrated by Barbara Cooney

Henry Holt and Company / *New York*

Published by Henry Holt and Company, Inc.,
115 West 18th Street, New York, New York 10011.
Published in Canada by Fitzhenry & Whiteside Limited,
91 Granton Drive, Richmond Hill, Ontario L4B 2N5.

Library of Congress Cataloging in Publication Data
Main entry under title:
Tortillitas para mamá and other Spanish nursery rhymes.
English and Spanish.
Summary: A collection of nursery rhymes, each in
both English and Spanish, collected from the Spanish
community in the Americas, many with instructions for
accompanying finger plays or other activities.
1. Nursery rhymes, Spanish—Translations into
English.   2. Nursery rhymes, Spanish American—Translations into English.   3. Nursery rhymes, English—
Translations from Spanish.   4. Nursery rhymes, Spanish.
5. Nursery rhymes, Spanish American.   [1. Nursery
rhymes, Spanish American]   I. Griego, Margot C.
PQ6267.E4N87   398'.8'0946   81-4823

Henry Holt books are available at special discounts
for bulk purchases for sales promotions, premiums,
fund-raising, or educational use. Special editions
or book excerpts can also be created to specification.

    For details contact:

    Special Sales Director
    Henry Holt and Company, Inc.
    115 West 18th Street
    New York, New York 10011

ISBN: 0-8050-0285-5 (hardcover)
10   9   8   7

ISBN: 0-8050-0317-7 (paperback)
10   9   8   7   6

Printed in the United States of America

INTRODUCCION

Estas rimas y arrullos fueron coleccionados de la comunidad Hispana en las Américas. Han ido pasando de generación a generación por padres y otros miembros de la familia quienes las oyeron desde niños y luego se las cantaron a sus propios hijos, cuando los detuvieron en el regazo o meciéndolos para dormir. Esas rimas familiares, llenas de calor, seguridad y amor, están coleccionadas en este libro para preservarlas para la comunidad Hispana y a la vez para darlas conocer a otros con su encanto.

INTRODUCTION

These nursery rhymes and lullabies were collected from the Spanish community in the Americas. They have been passed on from generation to generation by mothers, fathers, and other family members who heard them as children and later sang them to their own children as they held them in their laps or rocked them to sleep. These familiar rhymes, which kindle feelings of warmth, security, and love, are gathered in this book both to preserve them for the Spanish community and to acquaint others with their charm.

EL BESO DE MAMA

Todas las mañanas, sueño al despertar
Que un ángel del cielo me viene a besar.
Al abrir los ojos, busco adonde estoy
Y en el mismo sitio, veo a mi Mamá.

MAMA'S KISS

Every morning, I dream at dawn
That an angel from heaven will come to kiss me.
When I open my eyes, I look around
And in the same spot, I see my Mama.

RIMA DE LA HERMANA VESTIENDOSE

Pone, pone, tata.
  (Pon el índice en la mano.)
Mediecita para la pata.
Pone, pone, pon.
La manita en el botón.

SISTER'S DRESSING RHYME

Stay, stay, little sister.
  (Tap index finger on palm of hand.)
A little stocking for your foot.
Stay, stay, stay.
A little hand for your button.

CHIQUITA BONITA

Soy chiquita, soy bonita.
Soy la perla de mamá.
Si me ensucio el vestido,
Garrotazos me dará.

PRETTY LITTLE GIRL

I am small, I am pretty.
I am my mother's pearl.
If I soil my dress,
She will beat me.

RIMA DE CHOCOLATE

Uno, dos, tres, cho-
(Cuente con los dedos de la mano.)
Uno, dos, tres, -co-
Uno, dos, tres, -la-
Uno, dos, tres, -te
Bate, bate chocolate.
(Frote las manos como usa un molinillo
en una chocolatera.)

CHOCOLATE RHYME

One, two, three, cho-
(Count with fingers.)
One, two, three, -co-
One, two, three, -la-
One, two, three, -te
Stir, stir the chocolate.
(Rub hands together as if
using a chocolate beater.)

HALLANDO UN HUEVO

Este niño halló un huevo;
Este lo coció;
Este lo peló;
Este le hechó la sal;
Este gordo chaparrito se lo comió.

Le dió sed,
Y se fué a buscar agua . . .
Buscó y buscó . . .
¡Y aquí halló!
Y tomó y tomó y tomó . . .

(Cuente con los dedos para cada «este».
Busque agua primero en el codo,
después al hombro. Termine
haciendo cosquillas en la axila.)

FINDING AN EGG

This little boy found an egg;
This one cooked it;
This one peeled it;
This one salted it;
This fat little one ate it.

He became thirsty,
And he went to look for water . . .
He looked and looked . . .
And here he found it!
And drank and drank and drank . . .

(Count on the fingers for each "Este."
Look for water with the fingers,
first at elbow, then at shoulder.
End with a tickle under the arm.)

TORTILLITAS

Tortillitas para Mamá.
> *(Junte las palmas como aplaudiendo hasta el final.)*

Tortillitas para Papá.
> *(Se puede sustituir el nombre de los niños para Mamá y Papá.)*

Las quemaditas para Mamá.
Las bonitas para Papá.

LITTLE TORTILLAS

Little tortillas for Mama.
> *(Clap hands while chanting rhyme.)*

Little tortillas for Papa.
> *(Names of children may be substituted for Mama and Papa.)*

The burned ones for Mama.
The good ones for Papa.

LA MARIPOSA LINDA

Ayer que fuimos al campo.
Vi una linda mariposa.
(Ponga la mano enfrente de la cara
como si examinara algo precioso.)
Pero ella, al verme tan cerca,
Voló y voló presurosa.
(Haga otro ademán de volar.)

THE PRETTY BUTTERFLY

Yesterday I went to the field.
I saw a beautiful butterfly.
(Hold hand in front of face as if
examining something precious.)
But on seeing me so close,
It flew away ever so quickly.
(Make fluttering movement.)

LOS PESCADITOS

Los pescaditos andan en el agua, nadan, nadan, nadan.
  (Haga ademán de nadar con las manos.)
Vuelan, vuelan, vuelan.
  (Se puede aletear los brazos.)
Son chiquititos, chiquititos.
  (El pulgar y el índice juntos.)
Vuelan, vuelan, vuelan.
  (Repita movimientos.)
Nadan, nadan, nadan.

LITTLE FISH

Little fish move in the water, swim, swim, swim.
  (Swimming motion with hands.)
Fly, fly, fly.
  (Flap arms.)
Little ones, little ones.
  (Thumb and fingers together.)
Fly, fly, fly.
  (Repeat actions.)
Swim, swim, swim.

LA VIEJITA

Había una viejita,
   *(Los dedos suben el brazo despacio hasta
   la cosquilla rápido al final.)*
Juntando su leñita.
Llegó una lloviznita,
Y corrió, corrió para su cuevita.
   (Haga cosquillas en el estómago del compañero.)

THE LITTLE OLD LADY

There was a little old lady,
   *(Fingers climb arm slowly until the
   final quick tickle at the end.)*
Gathering wood.
It began to drizzle,
And she ran and ran to her humble home (cave).
   (Tickle your partner's stomach.)

COLITA DE RANA

Sana, sana colita de rana,
Si no sanas ahora,
Sanarás mañana.
(Se puede acariciar el golpe o lastimadura.)

LITTLE FROG TAIL

Get well, get well, little frog tail,
If you don't get well now,
You will get well tomorrow.
(Rub hurt away with circular motion.)

LOS POLLITOS

Los pollitos dicen «pío, pío, pío»,
Cuando tienen hambre, *(Toque el estómago.)*
Cuando tienen frío.
(Haga ademán de tener frío.)
La gallina busca el maíz y el trigo.
(Con las manos, busque los granos.)
Les da la comida, *(Toque la boca.)*
Y les presta abrigo.
(Póngalos debajo de los brazos para protegerlos.)
Acurrucaditos bajo las dos alas,
Hasta el otro día duermen los pollitos.
(Haga ademán de dormir.)

THE CHICKS

The little chicks say, "Peep, peep, peep,"
When they are hungry, *(Touch tummy.)*
When they are cold.
    (Make gesture for being cold.)
The hen looks for corn and wheat.
    (Make pecking motion in hand.)
She gives them food, *(Touch the mouth.)*
And she keeps them warm.
    (Make protective gesture with arms.)
Huddling under her wings,
They sleep until the next day.
    (Hand to head for sleeping gesture.)

LA LUNA

Ahí viene la luna,
(Ponga los dedos juntos en forma de la luna.)
Comiendo tuna,
(Pretenda comer con los dedos.)
Echando las cáscaras
En esta laguna.
(Haga cosquillas en el estómago.)

THE MOON

Here comes the moon,
(Form a moon shape.)
Eating prickly-pear fruit,
(Pretend to eat with fingers.)
Throwing the waste
Into the pond.
(Tickle tummy.)

ARRULLO

Duérmete mi niña,
Duérmete mi sol,
Duérmete pedazo
De mi corazón.
   (Arrulle al niño para que se duerma.)

LULLABY

Sleep, my child,
Sleep, my sun,
Sleep, little piece
Of my heart.
   (Rock the child to sleep.)

These pictures were painted for Gretel.